E
Fle   Fleishman, Seymour
        Too hot in Potzburg

$9⁵²

DATE DUE		
FE 8'89	AP 2'92	MR 14 02
JY 25	JY 1'92	AG 11 03
MY 2'89	NOV 05 97	JY 17 06
JY 12'89	FEB 23	JY 11'07
AG 3'90	MAR 17	JA 19 0
JA 4'90	APR 01 98	
FE 2'90	JUN 29 98	
JY 11'90	AUG 13 98	
AG 11'90	NOV 27	
JY 29'91	OC 31	
OC 14'91	0 26 00	
DE 23'91	E 23	
JA 16'92	JA 23 02	

MEDIALOG
Alexandria, Ky 41001

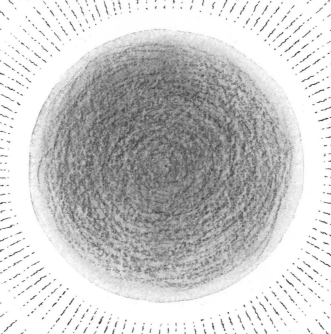

TOO HOT IN
POTZBURG

Story and Pictures by
SEYMOUR FLEISHMAN

Albert Whitman & Company, Chicago

For Esther, Jenny, and Suzy

Library of Congress Cataloging in Publication Data
Fleishman, Seymour.
    Too hot in Potzburg.

    Summary: One sweltering summer, Potzburg city
officials erect a giant electric fan, only to have
their plan backfire; while the fan blows away
the heat, it blows away everything else, as well.
    [1. Summer—Fiction. 2. Machinery—Fiction]
I. Title.
PZ7.F59924To   [E]   81-11498
ISBN 0-8075-8024-4   AACR2

The text of this book is set in sixteen point Palatino.

Summer came to the little city of Potzburg.
But this summer was not like other summers.
This time the sun felt bigger and redder
and hotter than ever before.

The heat was so great that
chickens laid soft-boiled eggs.
Bread toasted in the wrapper.
Paint melted off the houses.
Fish were caught boiled, ready to eat,
and corn popped right off the cob.

The citizens gathered at the City Hall to tell the Mayor how they were suffering.

"We cannot stand this terrible heat," they cried. "We citizens of Potzburg demand that you do something!"

The Mayor called the City Officials together.
"We must help the people," he said.
So they thought and talked for a long time.
At last the Chief of the Department of Heat, Cold,
Rain, and Snow came up with a plan they all liked.
"Wonderful!" they said. "That is what we will do."

Night and day the engineers made plans on their drawing boards. Day and night the machinery-makers made parts and put them together.

When the project was finished, the Mayor said, "Let's surprise the people." So late at night, when all the citizens were asleep, a giant machine was taken to City Hall, put in place, and covered with a great red cloth.

The next day the citizens gathered in front of
City Hall. The band played and the Mayor made a
speech. All the other City Officials made speeches, too.

Then the two Official City Cannons were fired to the
east and the west. The Mayor's young daughter, using
the Official Scissors, cut the ribbon that held up
the red cloth.

As the red cloth slowly floated to the ground, a great sigh of amazement came from the crowd. For there, on top of City Hall where the golden dome used to be, was an enormous electric fan—the biggest in the whole world!

"And now," shouted the Chief of the Department of Heat, Cold, Rain, and Snow, "plug in the Great Plug!"

The enormous blades began to turn, and the fan slowly revolved, pointing to the east toward Ezazza, to the north toward Noogle, toward Williwaw in the west and Shurdlu in the south.

Round and round spun the blades as the gigantic fan revolved.

Soon the citizens in all parts
of the city could hear the gentle
whir and feel the cool breeze
made by the spinning blades.
"Oh, how lovely it feels,"
they said. "Thank you, Mr. Mayor,
for driving away the
terrible heat."

After a while people noticed that the gentle whir was getting louder. Leaves and bits of paper were floating through the air. Birds flying toward City Hall seemed to stay in one place, no matter how hard they flapped their wings.

The whir became a hum, then a roar. The breeze became a wind. Hats and umbrellas filled the air.

Faster and faster spun the blades. Dogs, cats, and chickens were swept into the air.

People desperately held onto trees and posts.

Louder and louder roared the fan. The wind had become a hurricane!

Trash cans, furniture, trees, animals, and people flew through the air—eastward toward Ezazza, northward toward Noogle, westward toward Williwaw, and southward toward Shurdlu.

"Pull the Great Plug!" cried the Chief of the Department of Heat, Cold, Rain, and Snow.

After much tugging, the plug came out. The fan was stopped.

All was still, except at City Hall.

"The city is almost empty," cried the Mayor.
"We must find a way to bring everyone back."
The officials thought and worried and talked.
Finally the Secretary in Charge of Coming and
Going had an idea everyone liked.

New plans were made by the engineers who had not been blown away. Machine-makers who were still in the city made new parts and put them together.

The fabulous revolving electric fan was taken down and a new machine was put in its place.

The new machine was a gigantic revolving vacuum cleaner.

"This vacuum cleaner," said the Secretary in Charge of Coming and Going, "will suck back all that was blown away by the great fan."

The vacuum cleaner was switched on.
Humming loudly, it slowly turned, pointing
to the east, then north, west, and south.

Bits of paper and leaves were sucked in, then
pots, pans, small birds, cats, dogs, bushes,
trees, bicycles, horses, and all the people
and other things belonging to Potzburg.

"It's working, it's working!"
shouted the City Officials
as they danced about and
hugged each other.

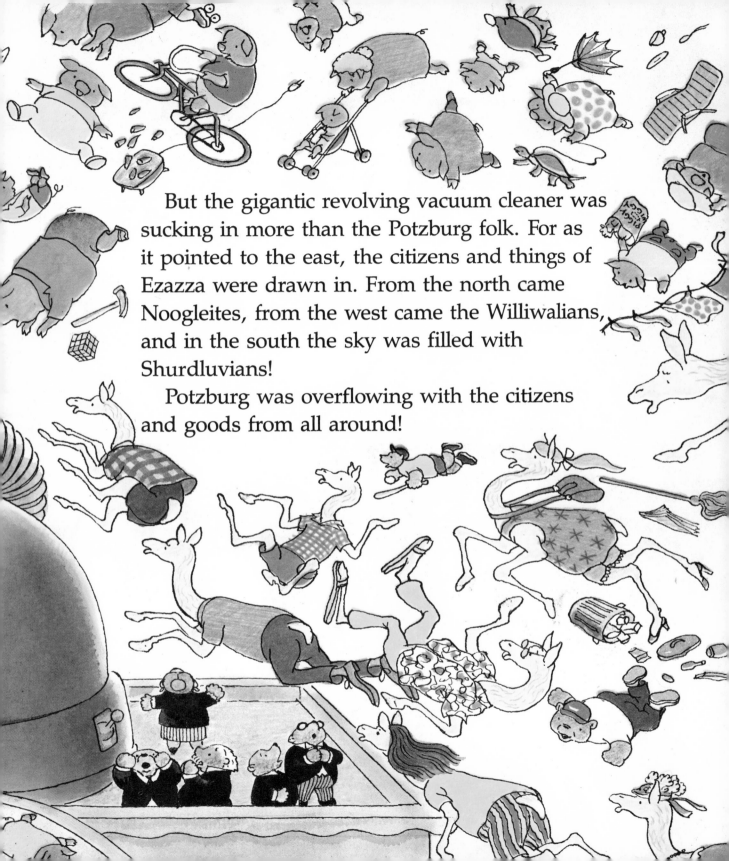

But the gigantic revolving vacuum cleaner was sucking in more than the Potzburg folk. For as it pointed to the east, the citizens and things of Ezazza were drawn in. From the north came Noogleites, from the west came the Williwalians, and in the south the sky was filled with Shurdluvians!

Potzburg was overflowing with the citizens and goods from all around!

"How dare you do this to us!" shouted the Ezazzans.

"We demand to go home!" cried the Noogleites.

The Williwalians and the Shurdluvians joined the angry shouters and shook their fists at the Potzburg officials.

Every wagon, cart, train, airplane, car, bus, bicycle, boat, wheelbarrow, buggy, and balloon in Potzburg was used to send all the angry people back to their homes.

Now green leaves were turning yellow and orange. Summer was ending, and the weather had become very pleasant.

The vacuum cleaner was taken down and the golden dome was put back on top of City Hall.

The electric fan and the vacuum cleaner
were put in the city park and made safe so that
children could play on them.

And for many years afterward, the people
told their children and their children's children
the story of that famous summer when it was
TOO HOT IN POTZBURG.